MYSTICONS

MYSTICONS

VOLUME 1

CREATED BY
SEAN JARA

STORY AND SCRIPT BY
KATE LETH

ART BY
MEGAN LEVENS
WITH **ANDY OWENS**

COLORS BY
MARISSA LOUISE

LETTERS BY
NATE PIEKOS OF BLAMBOT®

COVER BY
JEN BARTEL
WITH **TRIONA FARRELL**

PRESIDENT AND PUBLISHER • **MIKE RICHARDSON**
EDITOR • **SHANTEL LAROCQUE**
ASSISTANT EDITORS • **BRETT ISRAEL** AND **KATII O'BRIEN**
DESIGNER • **SARAH TERRY**
DIGITAL ART TECHNICIAN • **JOSIE CHRISTENSEN**

SPECIAL THANKS TO MARJANNE LYN, TALLY KNOLL, AND JEREMY KAPOSY.

Published by Dark Horse Books
A division of Dark Horse Comics, Inc.
10956 SE Main Street, Milwaukie, OR 97222

First edition: August 2018 • ISBN 978-1-50670-647-4

10 9 8 7 6 5 4 3 2 1
Printed in China

To find a comics shop in your area, visit ComicShopLocator.com.

Names: Leth, Kate, author. | Jara, Sean, creator. | Levens, Megan, artist. | Louise, Marissa, colourist. | Piekos, Nate, letterer. | Bartel, Jen, artist. | Farrell, Triona, artist.
Title: Mysticons / created by Sean Jara ; story and script by Kate Leth ; art by Megan Levens ; colors by Marissa Louise ; letters by Nate Piekos of Blambot ; cover by Jen Bartel with Triona Farrell.
Description: First edition. | Milwaukie, OR : Dark Horse Books, 2018-
Identifiers: LCCN 2018008196 | ISBN 9781506706474 (v. 1 : paperback)
Subjects: LCSH: Graphic novels. | BISAC: JUVENILE FICTION / Comics & Graphic Novels / Media Tie-In. | JUVENILE FICTION / Comics & Graphic Novels / Superheroes. | JUVENILE FICTION / Comics & Graphic Novels / General.
Classification: LCC PZ7.7.L48 My 2018 | DDC 741.5/973--dc23
LC record available at https://lccn.loc.gov/2018008196

DRAKE CITY. MULTICULTURAL HEART OF GEMINA AND HOME TO THE **MYSTICONS.**

THESE FOUR WARRIORS, SWORN TO PROTECT THE REALM FROM HARM AND GUARD THE MAGICAL DRAGON DISK FROM EVIL...

...ARE ALL FAST ASLEEP.

RMMMM
RRMMM
RMMMM
WHAT'S THAT?
AAAAH!
I'LL TAKE THAT, IF YOU DON'T MIND!
WHEEEEE!
VRUMMMM

HEY! STOP! YOU...YOU THIEVES!
ANYTHING GOOD?
UGH. NO. JUST A BUNCH OF...WHAT IS THIS, SPIDERBAT WEB?
WHAT A WASTE. TOSS IT!
RROAARR
C'MON. LET'S HIT A FEW MORE STREETS.
CATCH ME IF YOU CAN, SLOWPOKE!
ROAARR
IS NOBODY OUT THERE?!
HEEEEELP!

AAAH!

OH MAN...WHAT WAS THAT? WHAT...TIME IS IT?

NEVER MIND. IF THE SUN'S NOT UP, I'M NOT--

PREEEP!
AAAAH!

klik
WAKEY-WAKEY, ZARYA! WAS THAT YOU SCREAMING, OR DID SOMEONE SAVE OVER DOUG'S GAME AGAIN?
PREEE!
UNGH. NO. WAIT, WHY ARE YOU UP SO EARLY?
MALVARON'S HERE, AND HE BROUGHT PANCAKES!
PANCAKES? REALLY?

YES, REALLY.
WHAT'S THE CATCH?
MFORNIN', ZAWYA!

CAN'T A SOLON JUST DO SOMETHING NICE FOR HIS HUNGRY TROUPE OF COSMOVERSE-SAVING WARRIORS ONCE IN A WHILE?
THEY DO SMELL GOOD...

ALSO, MAYBE I WANT TO GIVE YOU A LITTLE PICK-ME-UP BEFORE I SHARE THE BAD NEWS.
THERE IT IS.

WHAFF OO YOU MEAM, BAB MEWS?
WHAT'S HAPPENED, MALVARON? IS IT DREADBANE? NECRAFA?
THAT'S THE THING--WE DON'T KNOW. I MEAN, WE DON'T THINK IT'S DARK MAGIC. HONESTLY, IT MIGHT BE A LITTLE BELOW THE MYSTICONS PAY GRADE.
ARE THOSE...PURSE-SNATCHERS?
DON'T YOU THINK THE LOCAL AUTHORITIES MIGHT BE BETTER SUITED TO SOMETHING LIKE THAT?
NORMALLY I'D SAY YES, BUT THEY'VE BEEN AFTER THESE TWO FOR A WEEK STRAIGHT AND NOBODY CAN CATCH THEM. THIS IS THE BEST PHOTO WE HAVE. THEY'RE LIKE GHOSTS.
ARE YOU SURE? I'VE MET GHOSTS. THEY'RE NOT THAT...NEON. OR FAST.
GHOSTS ARE SURPRISINGLY LAZY.
THEY STARTED OFF DOING SMALL JOBS, PETTY THEFT AND THE LIKE, BUT LAST NIGHT THEY HIT A SUPPLY SHIP AND MADE OFF WITH A KEG OF DRAGON NITRO.
HOLY GREMLINS THAT'S A LOT OF FIREPOWER!

WELL WHAT ARE WE WAITING FOR? WE'VE GOT TO STOP THEM!
WHEEK!
PANCAKES!

NOT SO FAST, ARKAYNA. NOBODY'S SEEN THEM IN DAYLIGHT AND WE HAVE NO IDEA WHERE THEY HANG OUT.
WAIT, COULD THEY BE HARPIES?
HARPIES?!
IT'S MORE LIKELY THAN GHOSTS. I'M TELLING YOU--LAY. ZEE.
THERE'S GOT TO BE SOMETHING WE CAN DO NOW.
LET'S HIT THE STREETS. IF THERE ARE NEW PLAYERS IN THE UNDERCITY, SOMEONE'S BOUND TO KNOW SOMETHING.
SOUNDS LIKE A PLAN. YOU NEED ANYTHING, YOU JUST GLYPH ME.
THEY MIGHT NEED A REFILL.

AAAAH, THE UNDERCITY! YOU EVER MISS IT, Z?
WHICH PART--THE SMELL OR THE HUMIDITY?
KEEP IT MOVING, PRINCESS!
WAIT UP, YOU =OOF= THREE!
OOH, SORRY. I MEAN... "PAL."
HEY, DON'T LAUGH AT ME! THIS WAS YOUR IDEA!
OH, WOW. THAT IS A *LOOK.*

I FEEL RIDICULOUS.
DO I HAVE TO HAVE THIS MANY LAYERS? I'M ITCHY.
YOU LOOK GREAT. BESIDES, YOU CAN'T GO ASKING QUESTIONS IN THE UNDERCITY WEARING A CROWN. MAKES PEOPLE NERVOUS.
CAN I HAVE A DISGUISE? I WANT TO BE A WITCH! OR A SNOW-GLOBE.

YOU'VE JUST GOT TO PLAY IT COOL. ACT CASUAL--
THAT'S THEM!
A CAT, MAYBE A CHINCHILLA? NO, DEFINITELY A ZEPPELIN.

WAIT, ARE YOU SURE?
MAYBE...POSSIBLY...I DON'T KNOW! LET'S KEEP AN EYE OUT AND NOT DO ANYTHING RASH.

RIGHT. GOT TO KEEP A LOW PROFILE.

HANG ON, WHERE'S PIPER?

EXCUSE ME! HELLO THERE! WOULD YOU HAPPEN TO BE COOL BIKER CRIMINALS?
OHHH MY GOBLIN.

WHAT'D YOU SAY?
YOU TALKIN' TO US, PIPSQUEAK?
AAAH! I MEAN, UHH...NO! NOPE. NEVER MIND. HAHA! WHOOPSY.
I'M JUST GONNA...

TOODLES!

WHAT IS SHE DOING?
INCOMING.
HUH?

IT WASN'T THEM!
WHAT WERE YOU THINKING? I DIDN'T COME HERE IN A DISGUISE FOR YOU TO GET US CAUGHT RIGHT AWAY!
YOU SHOULD KNOW BETTER, PIPES! THESE ARE YOUR STREETS, TOO.

SORRRRY. I JUST THOUGHT--
IT'S FINE. WE SHOULD SPLIT UP ANYWAY. COVER MORE GROUND.

"PIPER, YOU GO WITH ARKAYNA AND CHECK THE STREET VENDORS. MAYBE SOMEBODY SAW SOMETHING."
"WHAT ABOUT YOU?"
"I'M GOING TO CHECK IN WITH AN OLD FRIEND OF MINE."
SOUNDS GREAT! WHAT'S THEIR NAME?
YAAGH!
WHIIRP!

WHAT ARE YOU DOING? I TOLD YOU TO CHECK THE CHOP SHOPS!
YEAAAH, YOU DID. I'LL GIVE YOU THAT.
BUT THIS SEEMED MORE FUN.

WHERE ARE WE, ANYWAY?
AN OLD HANGOUT. IF THERE'S INFORMATION TO BE GOTTEN, THIS IS WHERE WE'LL GET IT.

SO LET'S GET IT GOT!

I'LL JUST...JUST GOTTA...PUSH RIGHT ON HERE, AND WE'LL...

THERE'S A TRICK TO THIS, ISN'T THERE?
MM-HMM.

HOLY HIPPOCAMPUS!
TRY TO BE COOL, OKAY? WE DON'T WANT TO CAUSE A SCENE.
I'M COOL! WHEN HAVE I EVER NOT BEEN COOL?
ALL RIGHT. HERE GOES...

WELCOME TO AMAKANTH.
WHOOOA.
STAY BEHIND ME. I'LL DO THE TALKING.
CAN I DO THE GAWKING?

WELL, WELL, AS I LIVE AND BREATHE. ZARYA MOONWOLF IN *MY* LITTLE ESTABLISHMENT?
HEYYY, BESS. HOW'S BUSINESS?

BRISK AND LIVELY, SAME AS ALWAYS.
STILL KEEPING OUT OF TROUBLE?
YOU KNOW IT. WHO'S THE SHORT STACK?

OH, HI. I'M EM. NICE TO MEET YOU! I'M--
THIS IS MY, UH...ASSOCIATE. ANIMAL WRANGLER.
IS SHE, NOW?
SURE THING. YOU WANT A FOZ? COUPLE KELPIES? SHE'S YOUR GAL.
AIN'T THAT SOMETHIN'.
IT IS! I'M ACTUALLY GREAT WITH GRIFFINS, AND--
SHE'S FUNNY, TOO. HAHAHA, SEE?
ALL TOO CLEARLY.

I DON'T KNOW WHAT YOU'RE UP TO, MOONWOLF, BUT YOU'VE BEEN OUT OF THE GAME A **LONG** TIME. PEOPLE TALK.
SAY YOU'VE GONE SOFT.
I THINK WE BOTH KNOW ***THAT'S*** NOT TRUE.

UHHHM...
I FEEL LIKE I'M MISSING SOMETHING.
AREN'T WE SUPPOSED TO ASK ABOUT THOSE BIKERS?
I KNEW IT! WHAT ARE YOU, COPS NOW? GET OUTTA HERE!
NO, WAIT! IT'S NOT LIKE THAT. WE'RE JUST--
♫ GIIIRL, CAN YOU IMAGINE--

WE'RE RIIIDING ON A DRAAAGON--
AWW, SNAP! THIS IS MY JAM!

YOU LIKE GNOMEZ 2 MEN?
DO I EVER! THIS IS THEIR BEST SONG!
OH, NO.
YOUR MAGIC TAKES ME HIGHER--

'CAUSE GIRL YOU LIGHT MY FAERIE FIRE!

AHAHA, AW MAN, Z! WHY DIDN'T YOU TELL ME YOUR GIRL WAS A GNOME-HEAD?
SHE DOESN'T GET IT! I'VE TRIED TO CONVERT HER, BUT SHE'S ALL, "UGH, WHAT IS THAT SOUND, MAKE IT STOP," ET CETERA.
CLASSIC ZARYA. NEVER COULD LIGHTEN UP.
THIS IS A DEAD END. LET'S GO.

LISTEN. YOU DIDN'T HEAR IT FROM ME, BUT IF YOU'RE LOOKING FOR WHO I THINK YOU ARE, YOU WON'T FIND THEM IN THE UNDERCITY. THEY HOLE UP IN THE JUNKYARD, THE ONE WITH ALL THE ORCS.
UH-OH.

THAT MEAN SOMETHING TO YOU?
NO, NO, JUST UH, GREAT SEEING YOU. RIGHT, EM?
YEAH! WE SHOULD HANG OUT SOMETIME, MAYBE LISTEN TO--
LET'S GO.

I CAN'T BELIEVE THAT WORKED.
WHAT CAN I SAY? I'M A CHARMER. LET'S GRAB PIPER AND ARKAYNA AND CHECK IT OUT!

I'M NOT SURE WE NEED TO DO--

--THAT.
LOOK! WE FOUND THEM!
WHERE HAVE YOU **BEEN?** I SENT GLYPH AFTER GLYPH...

RELAX, PRINCESS! WE GOT OURSELVES A LEAD.
"WE" IS A BIT OF AN EXAGGERATION, SEEING AS ***MY*** NATURAL CHARM SAVED THE DAY...
YOU KNOW WHERE THEY ARE?

CAN WE INFILTRATE THEIR GANG? WE'LL PROBABLY NEED BIKES, RIGHT? I COULD LEARN. CAN YOU TEACH ME? I'M PREEEETTY SURE I'D BE GREAT AT IT.

WHAT'S UP?
I THINK THIS IS GOING TO REQUIRE A LITTLE SUBTLETY. IT'S BIGGER THAN WE THOUGHT.

"THEY'RE WORKING FOR KYMRAW."
VRROOM
VROOOM
KISS MY TAILLIGHTS, *CLUTCH!*
QUIT WASTING YOUR NITRO, *THROTTLE!*
VRROOM
JUST 'CAUSE YOU'RE AFRAID OF A LITTLE SPEED--
YOU WANT A REMATCH?
WHERE ARE OTHER RACERS? THEY BEHIND YOU?
WERE THERE OTHER RACERS? IT SEEMS LIKE SO LONG AGO, I BARELY REMEMBER.
HAH! YOU WEREN'T KIDDING ABOUT THIS STUFF, BOSS. IT REALLY KICKS!

DRAGON NITRO NOT FOR PLAYING AROUND! IS TOO EXPENSIVE! IS NOT ENOUGH I LET YOU LIVE HERE FOR FREE?
UH, WE STOLE IT, AND YOU LIVE IN A JUNKYARD.
KYMRAW MAKE IT VERY CLEAR! I HOLD RACE, EVERYONE BET GOLD TO WIN, YOU WIN, KYMRAW GET PAID!
WE DID WIN. WHAT'S THE PROBLEM?
HOW KYMRAW GET PAID IF RACERS NEVER MAKE IT TO FINISH LINE?!
MAYBE YOU SHOULD TAKE THEIR MONEY BEFOREHAND.
NOBODY TELL KYMRAW WHAT TO--
THAT MIGHT BE GOOD IDEA, ACTUALLY.
RELAX, KYMMIE. WE GOT YOUR GOLD.
AND SINCE WE DID SO WELL, I'D SAY WE'RE OWED A SMALL CUT.
I NO THINK SO.

I HOLD RACE. I GIVE YOU DRAGON NITRO SO YOU WIN RACE. YOU WIN RACE AND GET ME GOLD. THAT OUR DEAL.
WE GOT THAT NITRO OURSELVES! THIS IS BOGUS, WE'VE DONE ENOUGH TO BE SQUARE!
HAH! YOU THINK WE ARE SQUARE? YOU THIEVING TWINS STEAL WHOLE SHIPMENT FROM KYMRAW! I LOSE MORE GOLD THAN I CAN COUNT!
TO BE FAIR, YOU AIN'T THAT SHARP.
YOU WANT SHARP? I CAN DO SHARP.
OKAY, WE GET IT! POINT MADE! WE'LL KEEP RACING.
YOU THINK NOBODY CAN CATCH YOU, BUT KYMRAW CAUGHT YOU. NOW WE TELL YOU WHAT TO DO.
HOW MUCH MORE UNTIL WE'RE PAID UP? WE CAN'T KEEP DOING THIS FOREVER. IF WE GET CAUGHT, WE ALL LOSE.
HMM...

WE HOLD BIG RACE. BIGGEST RACE. BUY-IN...10,000 COINS.
ANYONE CAN BEAT YOU TWO...I TELL THEM THEY WIN IT ALL.

BUT NOBODY BEAT YOU. EVERYONE LOSE.
AND THEY PAY *BEFORE-*HAND.

GO. SPREAD WORD. RACE IS ONE WEEK FROM TONIGHT. STARTS HERE. ENDS AT NEREID BAY. YOU WIN THIS ONE...
...THEN, WE SQUARE.
OH MY GOBLIN, THIS IS SO...
DANGEROUS? TERRIFYING?
INFORMATIVE? USEFUL?
SMELLY? WET FOR SOME REASON?
COOL!
THEIR OUTFITS ARE SO AWESOME AND THEIR HAIR IS SO BRIGHT AND THEY'RE ELVES JUST LIKE ME AND THEIR BIKES ARE SO...SO... GLOWY!
YOU REALIZE THEY'RE CRIMINALS, RIGHT? THIEVES? STREET RACERS?
WELL, SURE, BUT...
WE NEED TO GET OUT OF HERE AND FORMULATE A PLAN BEFORE--

VROOOOOM
EEEK!
COME ON! BOOK IT!

FAB. TACULAR.

"I SAY WE GO IN, GRIFFINS BLAZING! WE TAKE DOWN KYMRAW'S WHOLE OPERATION IN ONE FELL SWOOP!"
"WE'RE OUTNUMBERED THREE TO ONE, EM. IT'S TOO RISKY."
NOT AS MYSTICONS! ONE BLAST FROM YOU AT FULL DRAGON MAGEY-NESS AND POOF! PROBLEM SOLVED.
IT'S NOT THAT SIMPLE! WHAT IF THERE ARE MORE OF THEM? WHAT IF THOSE BIKERS AREN'T THERE AND WE BLOW THE WHOLE PLAN?
WE COULD ALWAYS TRY TO RACE THEM.
PIPER, THEY'RE RUNNING MAGICALLY SOUPED-UP MACHINES, AND EVEN IF THEY WEREN'T, NONE OF US KNOW HOW TO RIDE.
HEY, SPEAK FOR YOURSELF. I HAD A LIFE BEFORE THIS CASTLE, Y'KNOW.
YOU WANT TO TRY BEATING THOSE SPEED DEMONS ALL THE WAY ACROSS DRAKE CITY, BE MY GUEST.
RELAX, PRINCESS! WHY DON'T WE JUST TAKE THE GRIFFINS? EVEN DRAGON NITRO CAN'T COMPETE WITH IZZIE AND THE REST FOR SPEED.
NO. PIPER'S RIGHT.

IF WE WANT TO STOP THIS, I MEAN REALLY STOP IT, WE HAVE TO BEAT KYMRAW AND THE TWINS AT THEIR OWN GAME.
YOU CAN'T BE SERIOUS.

DEADLY. WHETHER THEY WIN OR LOSE THE ACTUAL RACE, KYMRAW'S NOT ABOUT TO LET THEM WALK AWAY.
SO WHY ENTER?

SHE'S GETTING AWAY WITH IT BECAUSE NOBODY'S WATCHING. AS SOON AS THIS GETS BIG ENOUGH TO DRAW ATTENTION TO THE JUNKYARD AND HER CREW, SHE'LL BACK DOWN.
ARE YOU SURE? SHE'S PREEEETTY TOUGH.
YEAH, I WOULDN'T PEG HER AS THE TYPE TO SHY AWAY FROM A SCUFFLE.

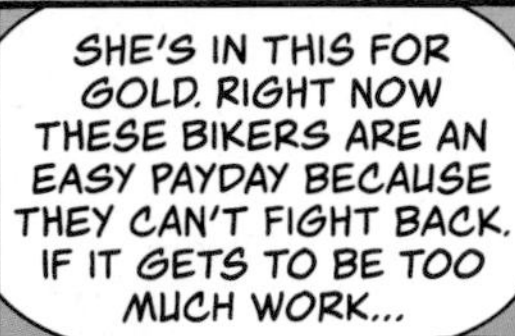
SHE'S IN THIS FOR GOLD. RIGHT NOW THESE BIKERS ARE AN EASY PAYDAY BECAUSE THEY CAN'T FIGHT BACK. IF IT GETS TO BE TOO MUCH WORK...

SHE'LL GIVE UP. FIND SOMEONE ELSE TO PICK ON.

EXACTLY.

IF YOU'RE SUGGESTING WE TEAM UP WITH THOSE CRIMINALS...
NOT EXACTLY. BUT I HAVE A PLAN.
THERE ARE DOZENS OF ROUTES BETWEEN THE JUNKYARD AND NEREID BAY.
IF WE KEEP WATCH TONIGHT, I BET WE'LL CATCH THEM RUNNING IT IN ADVANCE.
DOES THAT MEAN... IT'S *MAGIC HOUR?*
YOU BET YOUR BOOTS, PRINCESS.
FINALLY!
SORRY I'M LATE FOR THE MEETING, BUT I BROUGHT DONUTS! DID I MISS--
--ANYTHING?
NO TIME! GOT A LEAD!
WE'LL GLYPH YOU ABOUT IT LATER!
BYE-EE!
POP BY ANY TIME!

MYSTICON DRAGON MAGE!
MYSTICON RANGER!

MYSTICON
STRIKER!

MYSTICON
KNIGHT!

SPLIT UP, MYSTICONS! KEEP YOUR EYES PEELED!

NOTHING UP HERE SO FAR. EM?

NADA. QUITE A VIEW FROM HERE, THOUGH! DID YOU KNOW THERE ARE TWO SUSHI BURRITO PLACES ON HEXINGTON AVENUE?

ALL CLEAR UPTOWN, TOO. PIPER, WHAT'S YOUR STATUS?

10-4, GOOD BUDDY!
AAAH!

PIPER, WHAT ARE YOU DOING? WE SAID SPLIT UP!
I DID!
WITH YOU!

NO, I MEANT--
HEY, Z! I'VE GOT A VISUAL! MIDTOWN, HEADED UP IT!
YOU SURE?
PREEETTY POSITIVE.

EAT MY DRAGON DUST, BABY SISTER!
YOU'RE THREE MINUTES OLDER THAN ME, BRAT!
UROOOM
EXACTLY! RESPECT YOUR ELDERS!
I SEE YOU, THROTTLE! NO CHEATING!
AFRAID YOU'LL GET LEFT BEHIND?
IF YOU HAVE TO USE KYMRAW'S BOOST TO BEAT ME, YOU'RE A WORSE RACER THAN I THOUGHT.

ALL RIGHT, CALM DOWN. I'LL SAVE THE NITRO FOR RACE DAY.
KYMRAW SAID IT WAS FINE IN SMALL QUANTITIES.
IT'S NOT JUST THAT, YOU DINGBAT. THIS STUFF IS UNSTABLE.
I TRUST THAT TROLL ABOUT AS FAR AS I CAN THROW HER.
JUST DON'T WASTE IT TRYING TO BEAT MY TIME, THAT'S ALL.
I'VE BESTED YOU PLENTY.
=PFF!= I LET YOU WIN.
ALL I'M SAYING IS--WATCH IT. WE'RE SO CLOSE TO BEING OUT. ALL WE HAVE TO DO--
WHOOMF
WHOOMF
DID YOU JUST SEE THAT?

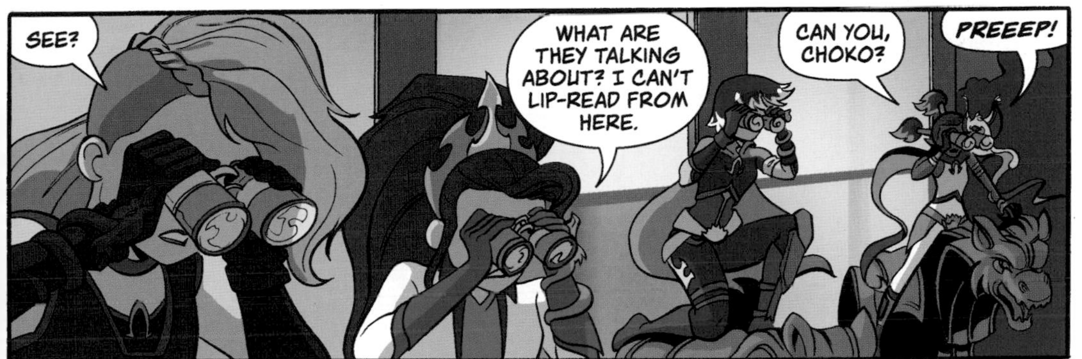
SEE?
WHAT ARE THEY TALKING ABOUT? I CAN'T LIP-READ FROM HERE.
CAN YOU, CHOKO?
PREEEP!

HE'S GOT NOTHIN'.

WE'VE GOT THEM CORNERED. LET'S MOVE.
WE CAN'T!

WHY NOT? YOUR MYSTERIOUS PLAN IS GREAT AND ALL, BUT THE BAD GUYS ARE LITERALLY HAVING A GOSSIP SESH RIGHT BELOW US. THIS IS WHAT WE DO!
PRINCESS--

WE'VE GOT TO STOP THEM.
I KNOW WHAT I'M DOING!
THEN SHARE WITH THE REST OF THE CLASS!

UH, GUYS?

THEY'RE GONE.

HOW COULD YOU LET THIS HAPPEN?

ME?! YOU'RE THE ONE WHO WANTED TO SIT AROUND AND LET THEM GET AWAY!
WE CAME UP HERE TO TRACK THEM, NOT TO--
HEY! ARE YOU THREE COMING OR WHAT?
PIPER!
AW YEAH, PIPES!

WHEEEE!
THEY ARE FOLLOWING US!
WHO IS?
WHOEVER THEY ARE, THEY'VE GOT GRIFFINS! WE NEED TO SHAKE 'EM!
DESPERATE TIMES.
HEY, NO FAIR!

PIPER, WHAT ARE YOU DOING? YOU'LL GIVE US AWAY!
I THINK IT MIIIIGHT BE TOO LATE FOR THAT.
I TOLD YOU WE SHOULD HAVE MADE A MOVE!
YOU GUYS--
BOOOM
THROTTLE!
WAKE UP! SIS, COME ON! WHAT HAPPENED?!

MYSTICONS.
IS SHE ALL RIGHT? WE HEARD SOMETHING GO BOOM!
DESPITE WHAT YOU MAY THINK, WE'RE HERE TO--

--HELP.

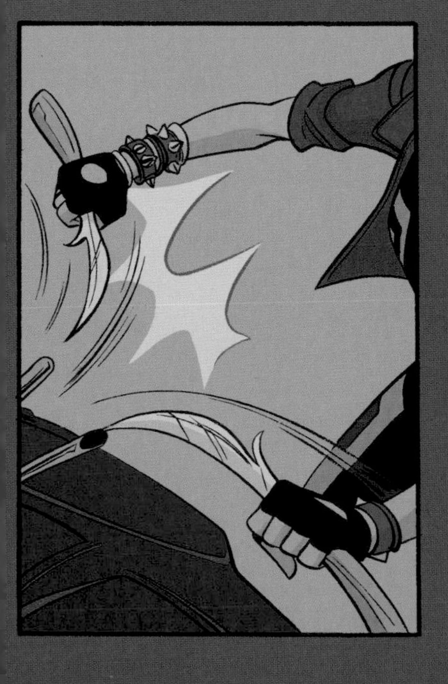

YOU'LL PAY FOR THIS!

HEY, NO, WE DIDN'T--

NYAH!

WE DIDN'T CAUSE THAT EXPLOSION! SHE MUST HAVE CRASHED!
THROTTLE DOESN'T CRASH!

GET AWAY FROM MY SISTER.

CLUTCH!

LET'S GO.

THIS ISN'T OVER, MYSTICONS!
URROOOM

LET'S GO! WE CAN CATCH THEM!
NO.

WE KNOW WHICH ROUTE THEY'RE TAKING. WE GOT WHAT WE NEEDED.
HOW CAN THEY EVEN RACE? ONE OF THEIR BIKES BLEW UP!
AND THEY THINK **WE** DID IT!
YOU COULD POWER A ZEPPELIN WITH HALF THIS DRAGON NITRO. WHY OVERCLOCK THE BIKES THIS MUCH?
IF YOU ONLY CARED ABOUT WINNING AND WEREN'T IN ANY DANGER...

OR IF YOU HAD AN ULTERIOR MOTIVE.
KYMRAW SET THEM UP? HOW? WHY?
SHE ONLY NEEDS ONE OF THEM TO WIN.
MAYBE SHE'S TRYING TO TIE UP LOOSE ENDS IN THE PROCESS.
THOSE RACERS ARE IN MORE TROUBLE THAN WE THOUGHT.

KYMRAW! WAKE UP! WE'VE GOT TROUBLE!
YOU BOTH MADE IT?!
AH-HAH, I MEAN, WHAT HAPPENED? KYMRAW WAS WORRIED!

WE WERE RUNNING THE ROUTE WHEN WE GOT INTERCEPTED BY MYSTICONS. THROTTLE'S BIKE IS TOTALED. THEY MUST HAVE HIT ONE OF THE TANKS.
STUPID... MAGICAL... GIRLS...
OH, UH, YES! THAT WHAT HAPPENED!

WE'LL HAVE TO CALL THE RACE OFF. I WON'T DO IT WITHOUT MY SISTER.
IS VERY SAD ACCIDENT, BUT YOU STILL HAVE BIKE...AND YOU STILL OWE GOLD.
IT'S NOT SAFE! I THOUGHT THAT NITRO WOULD GIVE US AN EDGE, BUT IT'S TOO DANGEROUS. IF WE RACE, WE RACE CLEAN.
I WANT ONE OF YOUR BIKES.
FINE. YOU TAKE HIS.
...HEY!
WHY IS EVERYONE YELLING? IS IT SLEEPYTIME?
I GOT YOU, KID. C'MON. LET'S MAKE SURE YOU'RE ALL RIGHT.

CHOOSE YOUR FIGHTER!
WELL, THAT DID NOT GO GREAT.

GAME OVER!
ONE THING'S FOR SURE...I'M DEFINITELY ENTERING THAT RACE.

YOU CAN'T! LOOK WHAT HAPPENED TO SOMEONE KYMRAW WANTS TO KEEP AROUND.
PLUS, THEY'VE ALREADY SEEN US. NO WAY YOU'D EVEN MAKE IT TO THE STARTING LINE.

CHOOSE YOUR FIGHTER!
NOT IF THEY DON'T RECOGNIZE ME.

GAME OVER!
...I'M READY TO SLEEP THIS OFF. I'LL LOOK IN THE ARMORY TOMORROW AND SEE IF ANY OF THOSE HOVER BIKES ARE EVEN STILL FUNCTIONING.

EM'S RIGHT. IT'S BEDTIME FOR THIS WARRIOR.
AW, MAN! I WANTED TO PLAY GAMES!
BEAT THIS BOSS AND YOU CAN STAY UP AS LATE AS YOU WANT!

SHE'S GOT A POINT, KID. LET'S GET OUR HEADS BACK IN THE GAME AND TALK THIS OUT TOMORROW.
YOU, TOO?!
I'VE GOT TOO MANY MOMS.

NIGHT!
DON'T LET THE BED-GOBLINS BITE!
HMPH!

"FINE. BUT I'M SLEEPING IN."
klik

FINALLY.

ZZZZZZZZ
VRRRRROOM

HNNKKKK ZZZZZZ

VRROOOOOM

HEY, KYMRAW! WAKE UP!
HUH? WHA--?

WHO WAKE UP KYMRAW? WAS HAVING NICE DREAM!

WE'VE GOT UNFINISHED BUSINESS.

WHAT TIME IS IT?
WHO ARE YOU?

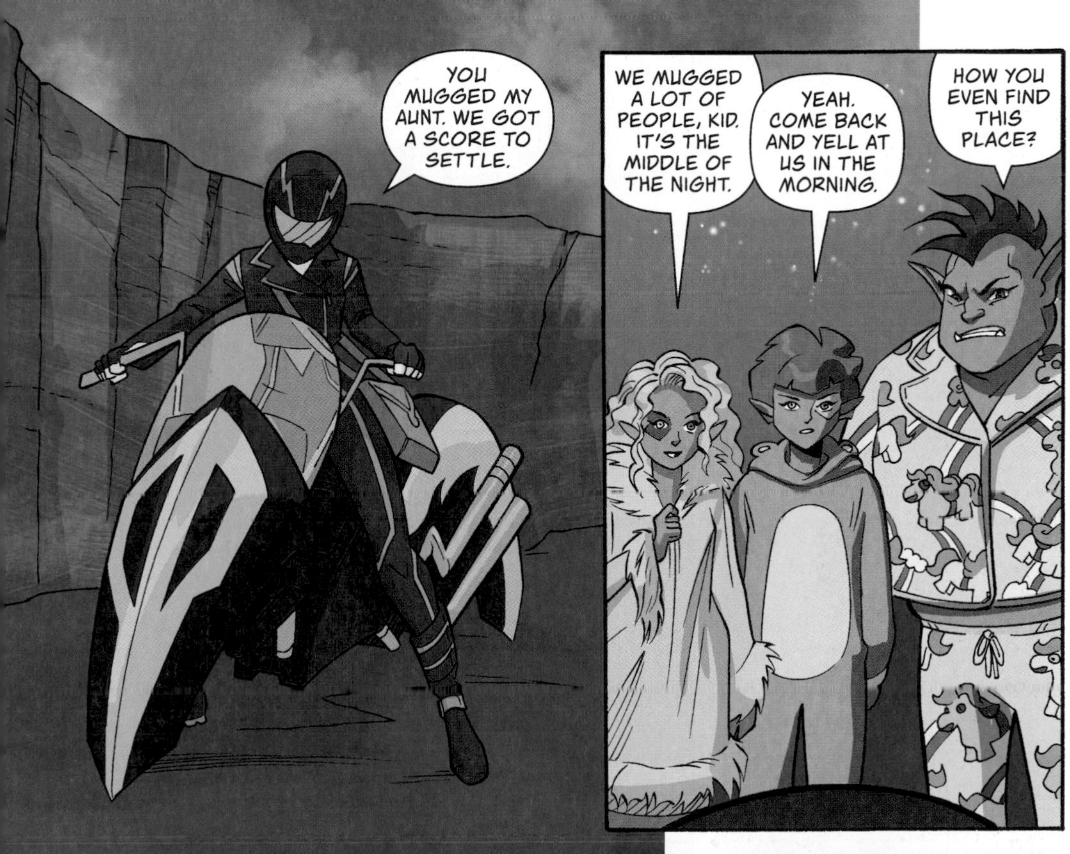
YOU MUGGED MY AUNT. WE GOT A SCORE TO SETTLE.
WE MUGGED A LOT OF PEOPLE, KID. IT'S THE MIDDLE OF THE NIGHT.
YEAH. COME BACK AND YELL AT US IN THE MORNING.
HOW YOU EVEN FIND THIS PLACE?

I'VE GOT EYES ALL OVER THIS CITY. I KNOW THE RACE YOU'RE PLANNING, AND I'M HERE TO CALL IT OFF.
HAH! FAT CHANCE YOU HAVE!

YOU'RE RACING FOR GOLD. I CAN OFFER SOMETHING BETTER.

THE DRAGON DISK.

WHERE YOU GET THAT?
YOUR TWINS AREN'T THE ONLY PICKPOCKETS IN TOWN.

WHAT YOU WANT FOR IT?
I WANT TO RACE.

BY MORNING, THE MYSTICONS ARE GOING TO REALIZE THEIR PRECIOUS DISK IS MISSING. WE DO THIS TONIGHT.
YOU WIN, YOU GET IT. I TAKE OFF, NO QUESTIONS ASKED.
I WIN, YOU CALL OFF THE RACES AND STEER CLEAR OF DRAKE CITY.

THAT'S IT? YOU WANT US TO GET LOST?
THIS IS MY TERRITORY.
THEN HOW COME WE AIN'T SEEN YOU?

I DIDN'T WANT YOU TO.

RACE STARTS AT PEGASUS PARK. TWENTY MINUTES.
WHAT YOU WAITING FOR? CATCH THEM!
BUT YOU SAID--

YOU GET THAT DISK, WE SQUARE. KYMRAW DON'T CARE HOW.
FINE BY ME.
Y'KNOW...

...YOU'RE A LITTLE LESS SCARY IN YOUR TWINKLY MARE PAJAMAS.

GO!

MAYBE SHE WON'T COME, ZARYA. MAYBE THIS WAS A BAD IDEA. MAYBE YOU SHOULD HAVE TOLD THE OTHERS.

VROOOM

I'M HERE. WE DOING THIS?
HI. HEY. LISTEN, CLUTCH, WAS IT?
WHAT'S IT TO YOU?
WE NEED TO TALK.

WE'RE NOT THE ONES WHO ATTACKED YOUR SISTER. KYMRAW IS--

MYSTICON?

YOU ATTACKED MY SISTER!
WHAT THE--WHERE DID YOU GET THAT?!

YOU WOULDN'T BELIEVE WHAT SOME PEOPLE THROW AWAY.
WAIT, LISTEN!

WHOOSH
VROOOOM
OR NOT!

VROOOM
VRROOMM

GET BACK HERE!
I'M TRYING TO HELP YOU!

HELP *THIS!*

HAH!

NO!

WOO-HOOO! GOT IT!
NICE ONE, PIPES!
I'M GETTING IT! I THINK I CAN ACTUALLY DRIVE THIS THING!
OH, PERFECT.

WHAT ARE YOU DOING?! I HAVE THIS UNDER CONTROL!
WE'RE HERE TO HELP YOU!
AND GET THE DRAGON DISK BACK, APPARENTLY!
I CAN'T--AH!--BELIEVE YOU--OH BOY--STOLE IT! AGAIN!
I HAD TO! THIS WAS THE PLAN! YOU NEVER TRUST ME TO--
AAH!
WHAM

ZARYA!
SKREEEE
KYMRAW?

GOOD RACE, MYSTICONS. IS OVER. NOW YOU HAND OVER DRAGON DISK.
NO WAY!
YOU'RE OUT-NUMBERED, KYMRAW.

MAYBE. BUT KYMRAW HAVE FIREPOWER.

ARE YOU NUTS? YOU'LL BLOW US ALL UP!

IT NOT FOR MY BIKE.

YOU MONSTER!

NOT MONSTER. ONLY TROLL.

NOW, MYSTICONS. HAND OVER DISK. KYMRAW NOT WANT TO SEE ANYONE GET HURT.

AAH!

THEN YOU SHOULD PROBABLY LOOK AWAY.

MYSTICONS! I DESTROY YOU JUST LIKE I DESTROY--
HEY. YOU.
I THINK YOU LEFT THIS FOR ME.
UH, MUST BE MISTAKE. IS NOT MY BIKE. ANYONE COULD HAVE PUT THAT THERE!
WHY DO I THINK YOU'RE NOT BEING TOTALLY HONEST WITH ME?
SHE HAD THIS IN HER POCKET.
FANCY THAT. A REMOTE DETONATOR.
I GUESS YOU WERE TELLING THE TRUTH.
WELL, DUH!
PIPER!
WHAT? SHE TELLS IT LIKE IT IS!

HOW ABOUT YOU AND I AGREE THAT AS OF RIGHT NOW, WE'RE SQUARE.
WE SQUARE! WE ANY SHAPE YOU WANT!

I'M GOING TO GIVE YOU A ONE MINUTE HEAD START. YOU BETTER HOPE I DON'T CATCH YOU.

YOU NO HAVE TO TELL ME TWICE!
MYSTICONS, AFTER HER!
NO.

I KNOW WE DON'T KNOW EACH OTHER, BUT I HAVE A FEELING YOU'LL UNDERSTAND. I HAVE TO DO THIS.
FOR MY SISTER.
YOU'RE MORE THAN WELCOME TO TRY AND KEEP UP!
WHAT ARE WE WAITING FOR? COME ON!
YOU'RE LETTING **BOTH** OF THEM GO?

I'M SORRY I RAN OFF. I THOUGHT I COULD HANDLE IT.
WE JUST WANT TO HELP. WE'RE A ***FAMILY,*** ZARYA.
YOU WERE RIGHT. IT WAS NOT A ***GREAT*** PLAN.
YOU ***HAVE*** HAD BETTER ONES.

AWWW, YOU GUYS!
NOT TO RUSH YOU OR ANYTHING, BUT THEY'RE GETTING AWAY.

YOU'RE RIGHT. WE'VE GOT THE DISK, WHICH YOU AND I WILL TALK ABOUT LATER--
YEP, YES, I EXPECT SO.
BUT THEY'RE STILL A THREAT TO DRAKE CITY.

"WHERE DO YOU THINK THEY'LL GO?"

"NOT SURE, BUT WE'LL NEVER CATCH EITHER OF THEM ON THESE BIKES.

"THEY'RE TOO FAST."

SO, WHAT DO WE DO?
WHAT WE SHOULD'VE DONE AAAGES AGO...
BUT WE HAVE TO COME BACK FOR THESE. WE WERE *DEFINITELY* NOT SUPPOSED TO TAKE THEM FROM THE CASTLE.
FWEEEEET!

FAB*TACULAR!*
NOW *THIS,* I CAN DRIVE.
COME ON, MYSTICONS.

LET'S SAVE THE DAY.
THE END

Clutch and Throttle designs by Megan Levens.

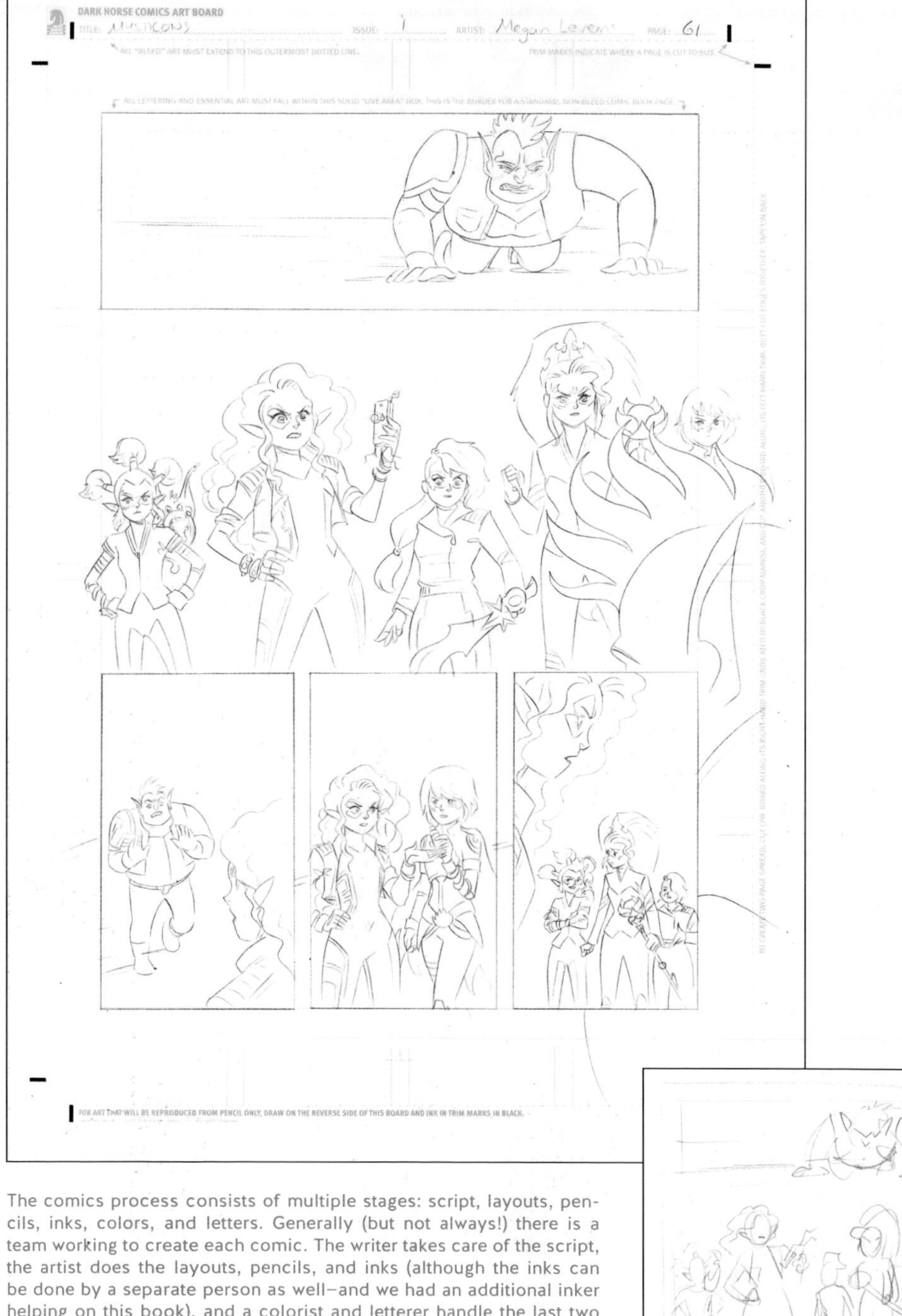

The comics process consists of multiple stages: script, layouts, pencils, inks, colors, and letters. Generally (but not always!) there is a team working to create each comic. The writer takes care of the script, the artist does the layouts, pencils, and inks (although the inks can be done by a separate person as well—and we had an additional inker helping on this book), and a colorist and letterer handle the last two stages to help create the final product.

Layouts are the first art stage of creating a comic. The artist uses this stage to help layout the panels and overall story flow based off the provided script.

Pencils are the next stage and are much more refined and detailed than the layouts, focusing on developing the characters and the actual images within the panels—including the smaller details called for in the script.

Inks are the last stage before the comic is colored and lettered. Here the artist is adding in the hard blacks and outlines. Compare to the facing page and the completed page 65!

Cover sketches by Jen Bartel.

Refined cover sketches of options A and D on the facing page.

Cover pencils.

Cover inks.

BOOKS THAT MIDDLE READERS WILL LOVE!

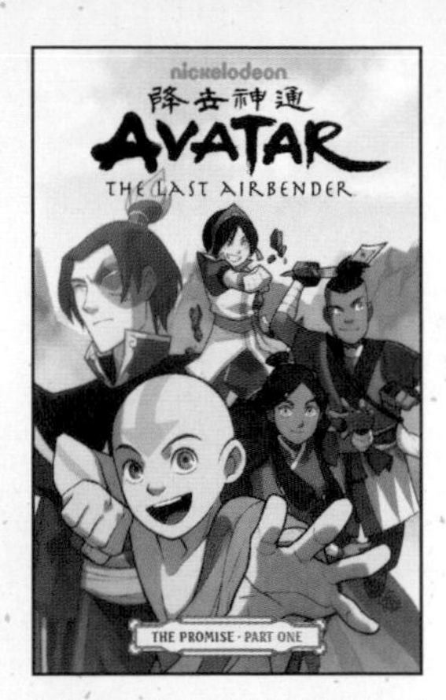

AVATAR: THE LAST AIRBENDER

Aang and friends' adventures continue right where the TV series left off, in these beautiful oversized hardcover collections, from *Airbender* creators Michael Dante DiMartino and Bryan Konietzko and Eisner and Harvey Award winner Gene Luen Yang!

The Promise ISBN 978-1-61655-074-5
The Search ISBN 978-1-61655-226-8
The Rift ISBN 978-1-61655-550-4
Smoke and Shadow ISBN 978-1-50670-013-7
North and South ISBN 978-1-50670-195-0
(Available October 2017)
$39.99 each

PLANTS VS. ZOMBIES

The hit video game continues its comic book invasion! Crazy Dave—the babbling-yet-brilliant inventor and top-notch neighborhood defender—helps his niece Patrice and young adventurer Nate Timely fend off a zombie invasion! Their only hope is a brave army of chomping, squashing, and pea-shooting plants!

Boxed Set #1: Lawnmageddon, Timepocalypse, Bully for You
ISBN 978-1-50670-043-4
Boxed Set #2: Grown Sweet Home, Garden Warfare, The Art of Plants vs. Zombies
ISBN 978-1-50670-232-2
Boxed Set #3: Petal to the Metal, Boom Boom Mushroom, Battle Extravagonzo
ISBN 978-1-50670-521-7 (Available October 2017)
$29.99 each

TREE MAIL

Mike Raicht, Brian Smith

Rudy—a determined frog—hopes to overcome the odds and land his dream job delivering mail to the other animals on Popomoko Island! Rudy always hops forward, no matter what obstacle seems to be in the way of his dreams!

ISBN 978-1-50670-096-0 **$12.99**

HOW TO TRAIN YOUR DRAGON: THE SERPENT'S HEIR

Picking up just after the events in *How to Train Your Dragon 2*, Hiccup, Astrid, and company are called upon to assist the people of an earthquake-plagued island. But their lives are imperiled by a madman and an incredible new dragon who even Toothless—the alpha dragon—may not be able to control!

ISBN 978-1-61655-931-1 **$10.99**

POPPY! AND THE LOST LAGOON

Matt Kindt, Brian Hurtt

At the age of ten, Poppy Pepperton is the greatest explorer since her grandfather Pappy! When a shrunken mummy head speaks, adventure calls Poppy and her sidekick/guardian, Colt Winchester, across the globe in search of an exotic fish—along the way discovering clues to what happened to Pappy all those years ago!

ISBN 978-1-61655-943-4 **$14.99**

SOUPY LEAVES HOME

Cecil Castellucci, Jose Pimienta

Two misfits with no place to call home take a train-hopping journey from the cold heartbreak of their eastern homes to the sunny promise of California in this Depression-era coming-of-age tale.

ISBN 978-1-61655-431-6 **$14.99**

DARKHORSE.COM

AVAILABLE AT YOUR LOCAL COMICS SHOP OR BOOKSTORE | TO FIND A COMICS SHOP IN YOUR AREA, CALL 1-888-266-4226

For more information or to order direct: On the web: DarkHorse.com •Email: mailorder@darkhorse.com •Phone: 1-800-862-0052 Mon.–Fri. 9 AM to 5 PM Pacific Time.

MORE TITLES YOU MIGHT ENJOY

ALENA
Kim W. Andersson

Since arriving at a snobbish boarding school, Alena's been harassed every day by the lacrosse team. But Alena's best friend Josephine is not going to accept that anymore. If Alena does not fight back, then she will take matters into her own hands. There's just one problem . . . Josephine has been dead for a year.

$17.99 | ISBN 978-1-50670-215-5

ASTRID: CULT OF THE VOLCANIC MOON
Kim W. Andersson

Formerly the Galactic Coalition's top recruit, the now-disgraced Astrid is offered a special mission from her old commander. She'll prove herself worthy of another chance at becoming a Galactic Peacekeeper . . . if she can survive.

$19.99 | ISBN 978-1-61655-690-7

BANDETTE
Paul Tobin, Colleen Coover

A costumed teen burglar by the *nome d'arte* of Bandette and her group of street urchins find equal fun in both skirting and aiding the law, in this enchanting, Eisner-nominated series!

$14.99 each

Volume 1: Presto! | ISBN 978-1-61655-279-4

Volume 2: Stealers, Keepers! | ISBN 978-1-61655-668-6

Volume 3: The House of the Green Mask | ISBN 978-1-50670-219-3

BOUNTY
Kurtis Wiebe, Mindy Lee

The Gadflies were the most wanted criminals in the galaxy. Now, with a bounty to match their reputation, the Gadflies are forced to abandon banditry for a career as bounty hunters . . . 'cause if you can't beat 'em, join 'em—then rob 'em blind!

$14.99 | ISBN 978-1-50670-044-1

HEART IN A BOX
Kelly Thompson, Meredith McClaren

In a moment of post-heartbreak weakness, Emma wishes her heart away and a mysterious stranger obliges. But emptiness is even worse than grief, and Emma sets out to collect the pieces of her heart and face the cost of recapturing it.

$14.99 | ISBN 978-1-61655-694-5

HENCHGIRL
Kristen Gudsnuk

Mary Posa hates her job. She works long hours for little pay, no insurance, and worst of all, no respect. Her coworkers are jerks, and her boss doesn't appreciate her. He's also a supervillain. Cursed with a conscience, Mary would give anything to be something other than a henchgirl.

$17.99 | ISBN 978-1-50670-144-8

THE SECRET LOVES OF GEEK GIRLS

Hope Nicholson, Margaret Atwood, Mariko Tamaki, and more

The Secret Loves of Geek Girls is a nonfiction anthology mixing prose, comics, and illustrated stories on the lives and loves of an amazing cast of female creators.

$14.99 | ISBN 978-1-50670-099-1

THE SECRET LOVES OF GEEKS

Gerard Way, Dana Simpson, Hope Larson, and more

The follow-up to the smash hit *The Secret Loves of Geek Girls*, this brand new anthology features comic and prose stories from cartoonists and professional geeks about their most intimate, heartbreaking, and inspiring tales of love, sex, and dating. This volume includes creators of diverse genders, orientations, and cultural backgrounds.

$14.99 | ISBN 978-1-50670-473-9

MISFITS OF AVALON

Kel McDonald

Four misfit teens are reluctant recruits to save the mystical isle of Avalon. Magically empowered and directed by a talking dog, they must stop the rise of King Arthur. As they struggle to become a team, they're faced with the discovery that they may not be the good guys.

$14.99 each

Volume 1: The Queen of Air and Delinquency | ISBN 978-1-61655-538-2
Volume 2: The Ill-Made Guardian | ISBN 978-1-61655-748-5
Volume 3: The Future in the Wind | ISBN 978-1-61655-749-2

ZODIAC STARFORCE: BY THE POWER OF ASTRA

Kevin Panetta, Paulina Ganucheau

A group of teenage girls with magical powers have sworn to protect our planet against dark creatures. Known as the Zodiac Starforce, these high-school girls aren't just combating math tests—they're also battling monsters!

$12.99 | ISBN 978-1-61655-913-7

THE ADVENTURES OF SUPERHERO GIRL

Faith Erin Hicks

What if you can leap tall buildings and defeat alien monsters with your bare hands, but you buy your capes at secondhand stores and have a weakness for kittens? Faith Erin Hicks brings humor to the trials and tribulations of a young, female superhero, battling monsters both supernatural and mundane in an all-too-ordinary world.

$16.99 each | ISBN 978-1-61655-084-4
Expanded Edition | ISBN 978-1-50670-336-7

SPELL ON WHEELS

Kate Leth, Megan Levens, Marissa Louise

A road trip story. A magical revenge fantasy. A sisters-over-misters tale of three witches out to get back what was taken from them.

$14.99 | ISBN 978-1-50670-183-7

THE ONCE AND FUTURE QUEEN

Adam P. Knave, D.J. Kirkbride, Nick Brokenshire, Frank Cvetkovic

It's out with the old myths and in with the new as a nineteen-year-old chess prodigy pulls Excalibur from the stone and becomes queen. Now, magic, romance, Fae, Merlin, and more await her!

$14.99 | ISBN 978-1-50670-250-6